W9-CPL-067

Fall Leaves Fun

Martha E. H. Rustad

Illustrated by Amanda Enright

LERNER PUBLICATIONS ◆ MINNEAPOLIS

NOTE TO EDUCATORS

Find text recall questions at the end of each chapter. Critical-thinking and text feature questions are available on page 23. These help young readers learn to think critically about the topic by using the text, text features, and illustrations.

Lerner Publications Company
A division of Lerner Publishing Group, Inc.
241 First Avenue North
Minneapolis, MN 55401 USA

For reading levels and more information, look up this title at www.lernerbooks.com.

The photos on page 22 are used with the permission of: Mark Herreid/Shutterstock.com (maple); MikhailSh/Shutterstock.com (pine); Maslov Dmitry/Shutterstock.com (buds).

Main body text set in Billy Infant 22/28.
Typeface provided by SparkyType.

Library of Congress Cataloging-in-Publication Data

Names: Rustad, Martha E. H. (Martha Elizabeth Hillman), 1975- author. | Enright, Amanda, illustrator.
Title: Fall leaves fun / Martha E. H. Rustad ; illustrated by Amanda Enright.
Description: Minneapolis : Lerner Publications, [2018] | Series: Fall fun (Early bird stories) | Audience: Ages 5-8. | Audience: K to grade 3. | Includes bibliographical references and index.
Identifiers: LCCN 2017061721 (print) | LCCN 2017057028 (ebook) | ISBN 9781541524934 (eb pdf) | ISBN 9781541520035 (lb : alk. paper) | ISBN 9781541527201 (pb : alk. paper)
Subjects: LCSH: Leaves—Juvenile literature. | Autumn—Juvenile literature. | Seasons—Juvenile literature.
Classification: LCC QK649 (print) | LCC QK649 .R87925 2018 (ebook) | DDC 575.5/7—dc23

LC record available at https://lccn.loc.gov/2017061721

Manufactured in the United States of America
1-44339-34585-1/2/2018

TABLE OF CONTENTS

Chapter 1
Looking at Leaves.....4

Chapter 2
Changing Seasons.....8

Chapter 3
Falling Leaves.....16

Learn about Fall....22

Think about Fall:
Critical-Thinking and Text Feature Questions....23

Glossary....24

To Learn More....24

Index....24

CHAPTER 1

LOOKING AT LEAVES

Let's go on a fall leaf hunt.

Leaves are colorful in fall.
Do you know why leaves change color?

Leaves have lots of tiny lines. They are called veins.

Leaves soak up sunlight.

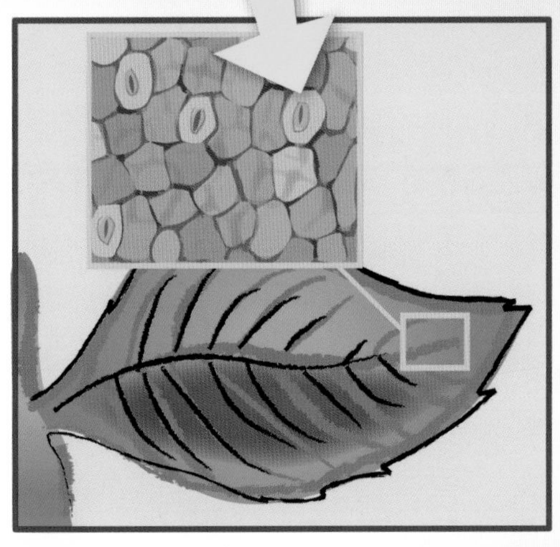

They take in air through tiny holes.
Leaves make food for trees.

Veins carry the food back to the tree.

What do veins do?

CHAPTER 2

CHANGING SEASONS

Trees change each season.

In winter, many trees have no leaves.
Trees don't grow during cold winter days.

Look! I spy a tiny bud on a branch.

Spring sunshine warms the buds.

Rain falls on the ground.
Roots soak up the water.

Look! I spy a little green leaf. Leaves unfold slowly from buds.

Bright summer sunlight helps leaves grow. Leaves are green in summer.

In fall, leaves stop making food.
Their green color goes away.

Leaves turn red, orange, and yellow.

What color are leaves in summer?

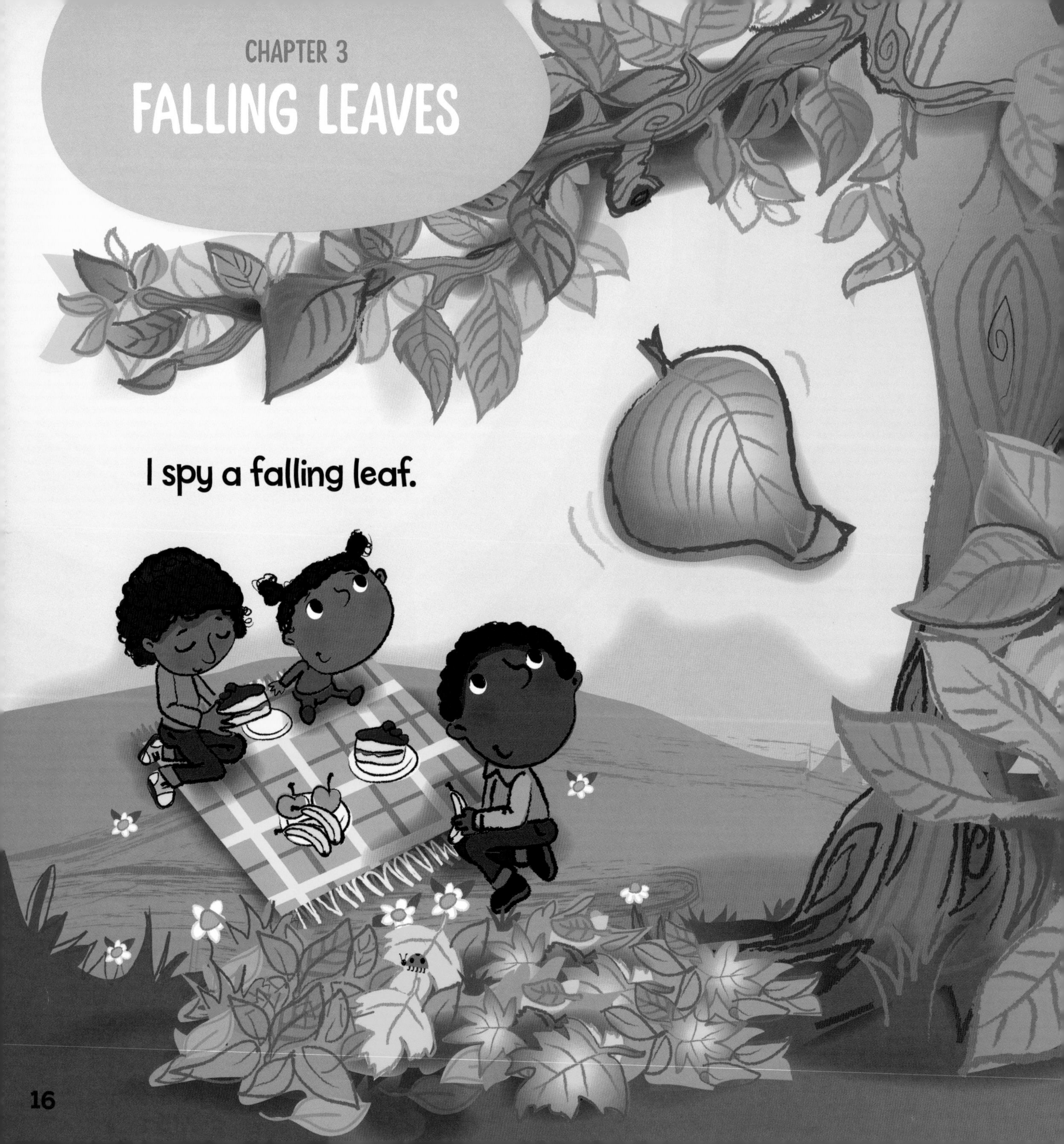

CHAPTER 3

FALLING LEAVES

I spy a falling leaf.

In fall, water stops going to the leaves. The parts holding the leaves to the branches grow weak. The leaves fall from the tree.

Crunch!

Dead leaves dry up and break apart.

Bits of the dead leaves sink into the ground.

These bits are good for growing plants.

Tiny scars are left on branches when leaves fall.

Near each scar is a small bud that formed during summer.

The buds wait all fall and winter.
In spring, leaves begin to grow again.

What happens to leaves in fall?

LEARN ABOUT FALL

When leaves make food for the tree, it is called photosynthesis.

Evergreen trees keep their green, needle-shaped leaves all winter.

Green bits inside leaves are called chlorophyll. They make food for the tree.

A tree's fall leaf color shows you what kind of tree it is. Maple trees have red or orange leaves. Birch trees have yellow leaves. Oak trees have mostly brown leaves.

During winter, bud scales cover the small buds. The scales protect the buds from getting too cold and dry.

THINK ABOUT FALL: CRITICAL-THINKING AND TEXT FEATURE QUESTIONS

Can you think of any other plants that change in fall?

What happens to leaves in fall where you live?

Who is the author of this book?

What do the numbers in the index mean?

Expand learning beyond the printed book. Download free, complementary educational resources for this book from our website, www.lerneresource.com.

GLOSSARY

bud: a small part that grows on a plant and becomes a new flower, leaf, or branch

root: a part of a plant that spreads out below the ground. Roots pull up water from the soil.

scar: a mark on a branch left after a leaf falls

vein: a tiny tube inside a leaf. It carries water to the leaf and food to the tree.

TO LEARN MORE

BOOKS

Griswold, Cliff. ***Fall Leaves.*** New York: Gareth Stevens, 2015. Learn more about how leaves change in fall.

Schuh, Mari. ***I See Fall Leaves.*** Minneapolis: Lerner Publications, 2017. Read more about colorful fall leaves.

WEBSITES

Activity Village: Four Seasons
https://www.activityvillage.co.uk/four-seasons
Show how trees change in different season with these coloring pages and activities.

INDEX

bud, 10-12, 20-21
spring, 11, 21
summer, 13, 20
veins, 6-7
water, 11, 17
winter, 9, 21